Sponsored by Children's Learning Museum

Published by Children's Learning Museum
PO Box 2598 Santa Cruz CA 95063

The Children's Learning Museum dedicates
this book to the development of all children,
encouraging them to reach their highest goal in life.

THIS BOOK IS PUBLISHED TO RAISE FUNDS FOR BUILDING THE CHILDREN'S LEARNING MUSEUM

ISBN 978-1-893931-04-6

Author: Franklin Marshall
Editor: Margot Nichols
Illustrator: Maricela Marshall
Designer: Erica Aitken

Festa was a cat. Festa was a cat who wore a coat. The first time you saw Festa, you would probably think, why is that cat wearing a coat?

In the daytime, Festa liked to go to the town marketplace.

He liked to see the shoppers.

He liked to see the beautiful market animals.

He liked to hide behind boxes or under pushcarts so he could watch without anyone noticing him.

Sometimes his hiding place was discovered, and he was chased away.

Being chased away always made him feel sad.

He wondered why people chased him away.
He wondered why other cats hissed at him.
He wondered why he was so different.

One day while Festa was hiding in the marketplace
enjoying the music and the beautiful animals…

...someone stepped on his tail by mistake.

Festa leaped from his hiding place with a yowl.

When he jumped up, he knocked over a display of apples that had been stacked in a pyramid. The fruit seller yelled at Festa and chased him.

Festa looked over his shoulder in fear, and ran into the table leg of a vegetable stand.

Vegetables flew everywhere.

Festa kept running.

Now he was chased by the fruit seller and the vegetable seller.

Other vendors tried to catch him.

Festa ran around and around the marketplace in circles.

His coat was just a blur as he ran faster and faster.

Everyone was trying to catch the cat in the coat.

Festa saw a goldsmith's stall and became airborne.

He sailed off the cobblestones and onto the goldsmith's table.

The goldsmith was so frightened, he threw up his hands and upset a small pot of melted gold right onto Festa's paw as Festa skidded to a stop on the table top.

Festa's paw hurt where the hot gold had stuck to his fur.

In one quick leap, Festa was on the awning that covered the goldsmith's table.

From there, he jumped down into a back alley and scurried away.

He could hear the angry voices of the market animals.

He could hear his heart beating fast.

He crawled into a box in the alley and fell into a
deep sleep.

Festa slept a long time. When he woke up he looked at his paw and it was covered gold!

He lifted his paw and looked at it.

What a beautiful paw, he thought. It's all shiny.

It's so shiny I can see my face in it!

"Oh, no!" Festa said out loud.

"Is that what I look like?

"I don't look like the beautiful cats at all!"

Festa licked his other paw, and ran it over his face.

He licked and licked, and rubbed and rubbed.

After a while, his face was clean and his whiskers perked up.

He looked at his reflection in his gold shiny paw.

He was surprised to see that his face shone like the sun.

And when he smiled, it shone like a hundred suns!

Festa sat up straight and looked at his tail that he had curled around his front paws.

His tail fur was in need of a good cleaning.

Once again, Festa licked his paw, and ran it over his tail.

He licked and rubbed, rubbed and licked.

After quite a while, his tail looked fluffy and clean.

Festa was pleased.

What about the rest of me? he wondered.
He held up his gold paw as if it were a hand mirror.
All he could see was the coat.

He took it off for the first time.

By turning his paw this way and that, he could see his chest fur, his back fur and tummy fur were all different colors!

He looked like a furry rainbow!

Is that who I really am? Festa thought.

Paw licking and fur rubbing followed.

Lick lick, rub rub.

Rub rub, lick lick.

Festa looked in his gold paw to see if he had missed any places.

He saw that his colorful fur was as clean and fluffy as it could be.

He could see who he really was and how special he was.

My, he thought, my rainbow fur is most unusually beautiful. I've never seen a cat quite like me—ever!

Festa decided to go back to the marketplace.
No one recognized him without his coat.

Not even the other cats who had always hissed at him.

They had never seen the real Festa before.

"What an unusual cat!" someone said.

"His face looks like a sunny day!" another person said.

"And best of all, he has a sweet smile!" the fruit vendor said...

44618666R10019